A MONTH
OF SUNDAYS

A MONTH
OF SUNDAYS

BY ROSE BLUE

Illustrated by Ted Lewin

FRANKLIN WATTS|NEW YORK|LONDON

FOR RICHARD AND RONALD

JEFFREY COVERED HIS EARS WITH HIS HANDS AND turned toward the cork wall. He pressed his face against last year's Little League trophy as the voices grew louder.

"Where did you get that lawyer of yours?" his mother was shouting. "I might have known you wouldn't leave before you gave me a little more trouble."

"Oh, turn it off," his father shot back. "If it wasn't for the kid I'd have gotten out long ago."

Jeffrey jumped out of bed and dressed quickly. His eyes felt full and his stomach felt empty. He had been feeling that way a lot lately. Each morning since Jeffrey could remember he had gone into the kitchen and eaten breakfast with his mother and father. Other men worked far away and rushed out early, but Jeffrey's dad worked right here in Lakeview and was always at the table every single morning.

It had been a week since Jeffrey got back from summer camp but it seemed more like a year. Now when Jeffrey woke up and went to the kitchen he would find his mother all alone, sitting at the table drinking coffee. There would be no eggs frying and no smell of bacon. Then his father would come in and the noise would start.

I

This morning Jeffrey didn't even want to pass the kitchen. He ran out the back door, got his bike from the driveway and walked it around front. He looked at the white house with the black shutters and the little streetlamp on the lawn reading 801 Hillcrest Lane. He looked away.

Jeffrey got on his bike and started pedaling. He was glad that the block was quiet. The street was empty except for a few people out walking their dogs and a few dogs out alone. Shep ran up to Jeffrey, barked at the bike, and wagged his tail. Some days you'd rather see dogs than people. Jeffrey reached down and petted his neighbor's dog. After a little while he pedaled on.

As he rode down the block that he would soon leave behind, he pedaled faster and faster. He wanted to ride so fast that all the houses, all the lawns, all the little growing-up trees, would be nothing but a blur. He kept his eyes on the rising speedometer and tried to see how far up he could make the numbers go.

Then suddenly a bell sounded and Jeffrey screeched his brakes and stopped. Just in time. As the gate at the railroad crossing came down, Jeffrey looked across the track. The platform was filled mostly with fathers. Jeffrey watched the

train pull in, swallow up the people, and head for the city. The gate went up and Jeffrey rode on more slowly now. Do they ride bikes in the city? he wondered. Would he get to keep his bike? He cut through the parking lot of the still-closed shopping center, turned the corner, and stopped at the door of School Number 7. The sign over the door said, "Through these doors pass America's hope for the future."

He walked his bike past the one-story block-long school, back past the tennis courts and the running track. He parked it in the bike rack and walked to the handball court. Soon the kids would be pouring into the yard of the closed school, but now it was deserted. Jeffrey sat down, his back against the wall of the handball court.

In two weeks School Number 7 would be open. Jeffrey thought back to June and the report card that told him he was promoted to Class 5-1, and that his teacher would be Mrs. Woodruff. But now he was going to a strange school, in a strange place.

"You'll love the city," his mother had said. "It will be new and exciting."

"I'll come to see you every Sunday," his father said. "We'll still be pals."

"Sometimes people find that they can't get along anymore and they stop living together. But they still love their children just the same."

Jeffrey tried to picture how it would be. A new school, a new city. His mother working instead of staying home. He tried to imagine it but his mind couldn't draw the picture.

He remembered the ride back on the camp bus. How he had wished the driver would hurry to Lakeview and how he had started feeling scared at the same time. How he had thought of home and back to last spring, back to the whispers in the night and the raised angry voices and the whispers again.

He banged his hand on the floor of the handball court. If only he hadn't gone to camp this summer. If only he had stayed home. Maybe he could have stopped this terrible thing from happening.

"Hey, Jeff," Wayne was saying, "you sitting here waiting for school to open?"

Jeffrey looked up and swallowed hard. "Hi, Wayne," he said.

Wayne plopped down. "Two more weeks and we'll be in there instead of out here. In there, listening to old Mrs. Woodruff."

Jeff looked down at the floor. "I won't be in your class," he said quietly. "We're moving, my mom and me." Jeff had kept it inside him for one whole week now, feeling too ashamed to tell his secret out loud. "We'll live in the city. My folks are getting divorced."

"Oh, yeah," Wayne said. "The city sounds great. You know Glen's folks split up last year, and Sandy's folks too. My mom says it's money all the time. You want to play some ball?"

Jeff shook his head. He had thought the news inside him would explode like an old warm soda-pop bottle when he finally let it out. But now he had said the words and Wayne hadn't even heard the shame.

"Hey, you guys sleep here or what?"

Jeff looked up and saw a bunch of boys standing over him. The yard was starting to fill up. Jeff and Wayne stood up, left the court, and walked their bikes toward the gate.

"You want to play tennis?" Wayne asked.

Jeff shook his head again.

"How about riding to your house?"

Jeff got a sick feeling in his empty stomach. "No. Can we go over to your house and get something to eat?"

"Yeah, sure. Come on. I'll race you there."

Wayne got on his bike and shot out. Jeffrey jumped up and pedaled hard. He caught up with Wayne and then sped past him. He looked back as the school and Wayne got smaller and smaller and the numbers on the speedometer got bigger and bigger.

Jeffrey and his bike were together a lot all that week. He polished his bike, oiled it, and held tight to the handlebars as he rode by houses with gardens, fountains, birdbaths, and little iron deer on the lawns. He stayed away from his own house as much as he could because every time he went home something else was gone.

First the hammock in the yard was taken down. Next, the pool table was missing from the recreation room downstairs. One day he came home to find the living-room furniture pushed away from the wall and covered with big white cloths so you could hardly tell it was a living room at all.

Then late one day he came home to find his own furniture gone. The whole house was filled

with shadowy shapes under white cloth. Nailed-up packing crates were everywhere. Jeffrey climbed over one and looked around his room. The floor was a carpet of crates.

He ran his hand over the cork wall next to the place where his bed used to be. The whole wall was like one big bulletin board and Jeffrey loved to tack things on it till it was nearly covered. Covered with record album jackets, pictures, old report cards. Now all that was left was the Little League trophy that somebody forgot to pack. Jeffrey lifted it off the wall carefully and sat down on a packing crate. He held the trophy tight and looked out his curtainless windows as the nighttime fell over his empty lawn.

Jeffrey spent that night at Wayne's house, and the next time he saw the packing crates they were piled high all over the New York apartment that he was supposed to call home. The cloth-covered furniture filled the rooms, like Halloween ghosts.

"Hey, kid," the moving man said, "you're standing in our way."

Jeffrey went to see the room that was to be his, but before he had a chance to look around, his mother and the moving men were there.

"Jeff honey," his mother said, "can you stand someplace else? You're in the way."

In the way. No matter where he stood he would be in the way. He ran out the open door and rang for the elevator. Jeffrey looked up at the lighted numbers. It took so long for the elevator to get from the first floor to the second that Jeffrey felt he couldn't bear to wait until it reached the eighth. He opened the door marked "exit" and ran down seven flights of stairs to the street.

He walked to the nearest corner and kept on walking. The houses here didn't all look alike the way they did in Lakeview. There were big apartment houses, some with doormen. some bigger than others, and right between them were small brownstone houses, old and dirty looking. All the houses were close together, standing next to each other with no room between them, like the people on the street. So many people. Walking on the street, standing around, sitting on the stoops of the little houses.

The people didn't look alike either. Some looked the same as the people in Lakeview, some looked different and spoke with an accent, and some were black. Most of the black people Jeffrey had seen walking on the streets of Lakeview were women who came on the morning train and helped in the houses.

Jeffrey came to a big street and crossed to the next corner. The street was so wide there was a little island filled with benches standing in the middle of the crosswalk. People were sitting on the benches. Jeffrey looked at them. Most of the people seemed very old. There were hardly any old people living in Lakeview. Jeffrey crossed to the other side and read the street sign. He was on Broadway. No wonder the street was so big. There were stores as far as he could see, and the streets were crowded with shoppers. There were food stores, supermarkets, and little groceries with signs he didn't understand. He wondered what BODEGA

and COMIDAS could mean. There were all kinds of clothing stores, big and little, and there was a movie house. Here you could walk to the movies. In Lakeview people rode to the movies in their cars. Nobody walked anywhere.

Jeffrey looked at the people to see if there were any kids his own age around here but he couldn't really tell. He thought of Wayne, of riding together, of sailing together, of the Little League, and suddenly he felt all alone on the crowded street.

The lonesome feeling stayed with Jeffrey all that day. It hung on the next day, too, till late in

the afternoon when Frank the doorman buzzed from the lobby.

"A visitor on the way up," he said.

Jeffrey went to the door as Dad stepped out of the elevator.

He felt like running to his father, but he just stood there. Dad put an arm around Jeffrey's shoulder, led him inside, and said, "How do you like the big city, pal?"

Jeffrey looked down. "It's okay, I guess. But I miss Wayne and Mark and the other guys. I don't know any kids here."

"You will, Jeff. School starts tomorrow and you'll make new friends before you know it."

Jeffrey thought of going to a new school and his stomach hurt. He had always liked school but now he thought of tomorrow and felt sick.

"Dad," he said, "why do I have to live here? Why can't I go to my real school? Why can't I live in Lakeview? We could go back now."

Dad rumpled Jeff's hair. "Now, Jeff, you know I'm living at Aunt Anita's till I find an apartment. And you know most children live with their mothers if their parents aren't together."

"I know. But Glen and his mom stayed in Lakeview. Why'd we have to leave?"

"Come on, pal. You know your mother's going to work in Uncle Jonathan's office. You'll love the city — you'll see! Now it's a beautiful Sunday. Let's get going."

"Can we go bowling?" Jeffrey asked excitedly. "Like we always did at Mapleton Lanes?"

"I don't think there's a place like Mapleton around here, Jeff. Let's do something really city. We'll take the subway and go to Radio City Music Hall. Then we'll walk around town and find the best restaurant in New York. Just you and me."

Jeffrey thought of Mapleton Lanes where you could bowl, have hot dogs and soda pop, and listen to the jukebox. He remembered how he went there on Sundays with his mom and dad, and he turned away. He didn't want his dad to see him sniffling like some little crybaby kid.

Jeffrey tried to act like he was having fun, but it got harder and harder as the day wore on. He looked at the big shiny stage with colors, lights, and noise and started to turn to his father. He nearly said, "Dad, could we go home now? I'm tired," and then he caught himself. He didn't have that home to go to anymore.

Night came at last, and when Jeffrey got back, his mother was reading in the living room. She jumped up and hugged him.

"Did you have fun?" she asked.

Jeff nodded.

His mother moved back and looked at him. "You must be tired," she said. "You've had a long day."

Jeffrey looked down and ran his toe round and round on the carpet. Then the words just spilled out — sad, mad, and puzzled all at the same time.

"Why'd he have to do that, Mom? Why'd he have to act like that? Going to all those places. Making me try and have fun all the time."

"Well, honey," she said slowly, "maybe your father was trying to do something extra exciting to make the day special for you."

"I guess so," Jeffrey said. "That's what Uncle Jonathan used to do when he came to Lakeview to take me out. He would bring presents and take me to lots of places all in one day. But that was Uncle Jonathan. It wasn't Daddy."

Jeffrey's mother put her hand on his arm. "You know, Jeff," she said, "maybe your father wanted to make the day special for himself, too, so he could remember it all week till next Sunday. It's going to be a little hard for you for awhile and for your dad and me too. For all of us. It will take time." She kissed his forehead. "And now, young man, it's time to get ready for bed. School tomorrow, you know."

The furniture in his new room was getting easier to see, and Jeffrey lay wide-awake knowing the morning was near. He felt bad all over. Maybe if he got sick he wouldn't have to go to school. Maybe if he wished hard enough the morning would never come. The light kept pushing its way into all the corners, and now Jeffrey could see nearly everything. The room didn't look too much different from his room in Lakeview. It was almost as big, and all his old things were here. All except the cork wall. His treasures were still in the carton near the closet. Jeffrey shut his eyes tight and wished he could go to sleep. He wished he could sleep for a long time and open his eyes in his old room in Lakeview. He slid deeper down into the covers as the alarm shrieked and his mother called, "Jeffrey, time to get up."

You could see the flag on top of the school from Jeffrey's corner. He walked slowly, slow as he could. The streets were crowded for this time of morning. Crowded and noisy. There were so many different sounds mixed together, like a stereo record. Horns blared, footsteps drummed the sidewalk, and people called to each other — some in languages Jeffrey did not understand.

Jeffrey looked up at P.S. 362. It didn't look anything like School Number 7. It was four stories high — tall and narrow, not all spread out like his old school. He walked around, looking for the handball and tennis courts, but all he saw were basketball hoops, a playground, and a big empty play area with no grass. The schoolyard looked very small. Kids had been lining up in the yard, and everybody was going in the side door. Most all the classes were gone, and Jeffrey followed the last class into the building. The card he held said Class 5-205. It was up one flight of stairs.

Jeffrey stood behind the second-floor landing and pictured himself running down the stairs. He could leave and run away. But where would he go? If he went back to Lakeview where would he stay? He could go to Wayne's, or Mark's, or Glen's, but their folks would call his folks and make him go home. He could try to stay with his dad, but there would be no room at Aunt Anita's and he would be sent back. There was no place in the world he wanted to be but Lakeview, so he found Room 205, walked in, and took a seat in the back near the window.

A man teacher was calling the roll. Jeffrey heard names like Pedro, Tyrone, Maria, Steven, Rosa, and Herbert. He looked around the room. There were all different kinds of kids, too, just like the names. Then the teacher said his name was Mr. Hart.

There were no teachers like Mr. Hart in Lakeview. Jeffrey had never had a man teacher before. Mr. Hart was younger than Dad. He had a red beard and lots of long red hair, and instead of a shirt and tie he wore a turtleneck sweater and a great big silver medal that said "Peace."

Mr. Hart started passing out books and Jeffrey looked out the window. He thought of Lakeview and dreamed about School Number 7 and Wayne and Mark. His eyes were open but he saw Class 5-1 and not Class 5-205. Then Mr. Hart's voice got louder and Jeffrey looked away from the window. Mr. Hart's voice rose, fell, got low, and then boomed. He used his arms a lot and kept moving all the time. He walked around the room, looking real cool. Jeffrey looked at Mr. Hart some of the time and out of the window some of the time, but as it got later, he looked out the window less and less.

Mr. Hart decided to go out for gym last period so he could dismiss the class from the yard. Some of the kids were throwing basketballs and Jeffrey joined in the game. Others were running, laughing, and talking, and then a boy said something to him. He spoke English with some foreign words mixed in, and Jeffrey couldn't understand him at first. He sounded like some of the people Jeffrey had heard speaking on the street. The boy started to get mad. Jeffrey still didn't get what the boy said, but he heard the name Santos and he answered, "My name is Jeffrey. Hi, Santa."

"Santa! My name is Santos, not Santa. It's Spanish, stupid. I ain't no Santa Claus."

The kid was getting madder. Jeff made out the words, "What are you, man, a joker or something?" and the next thing he knew he was lying on the concrete. He and the Spanish kid were rolling around the yard punching each other. And then Jeff got mad. He got mad at the kid, mad at New York, mad at his mom and dad, and he pinned Santos down and started punching him faster and harder and harder.

Mr. Hart pulled Jeffrey up with one hand and Santos up with the other and held them far apart, tight and strong. "Knock it off, you guys," he said in a tough voice. "Stand still and cut it out." He blew his whistle. "Class dismissed," he called. "I want to see you two in the room," he said. "Like right now."

He made Santos wait outside and he talked to Jeffrey first, alone. "Okay, Jeff," he said. "I want to hear what's bugging you. All of it."

Suddenly Jeffrey started talking and before he knew it he was telling Mr. Hart everything. All about Lakeview, and coming home from camp, and the divorce. Mr. Hart stayed quiet and listened,

and when he spoke he said a lot of things Mom had said, and Dad had said. Jeffrey figured he had heard all these grown-up words before and he started to tune out. And then Mr. Hart put his arm around Jeffrey's shoulder and said something he would remember for a long time.

"I know it seems like they're giving you a bad time, Jeff, but even if your folks split you've gotta stay together."

Mr. Hart told Jeffrey he could go home and called Santos into the room. Jeff never found out what the two of them talked about.

Next morning, while Class 5-205 lined up in the yard, their teacher rode up on a motorcycle.

All the kids ran out and crowded around Mr. Hart. He took off his motorcycle helmet and held it out to the class. Everyone reached for it, but Santos grabbed it and held it. He turned to Jeffrey.

"Gee, man," he said, "I didn't know you were a new kid. If I knew, I wouldn't get mad." He handed the helmet to Jeffrey. "You know, man," he said, "I was a new kid last year, too."

Jeffrey got to school early every day from then on. He waited to hear the motorcycle roar down the block and ran with the rest of the class to meet Mr. Hart. He started to feel a little better after that, especially in school. But after three he would go home to the empty apartment and many times he would dream with his eyes open. He would picture his family, all together, back in Lakeview, back on Hillcrest Lane. The dream was so real that many times he was sure it would come true. After awhile, he thought, they would see what a terrible mistake they had made. They would feel bad, just like he did, and they would all go back to live in Lakeview, and everything would be all right again.

There was a lot of time to dream after school. In Lakeview his mother was always home at three.

She would give him milk and cookies and sit with him while he told her about his day. Then she would start dinner and he would go out and play with his friends. When he came home the house always smelled good and dinner was always ready. Soon his dad would come home and they would all sit down together at the table.

Now there was no one to talk to when he came home and the apartment hardly ever smelled like a home at all. Instead of making special dishes, Mom would come in and usually defrost a TV dinner; or fix some vegetables and broil some meat, like hamburgers; or say, "Jeffrey, run down to the take-out place. I'm beat."

In Lakeview she always wanted to know what he was up to and sometimes she would be a big pest, asking him questions all the time. But now he felt she didn't care where he went or what he did. It was as though she was hardly ever home and when she was, she seemed far away, like she wasn't really there. His father seemed a little far away sometimes, too, when he came on Sundays. Jeffrey missed his father most of all. He used to be around much more than other dads in Lakeview because he worked so near the house. It was hard having a dad who loved you on Sundays when he used to love you every day.

Sometimes Jeffrey wished his teacher would give him more homework so he wouldn't have so much time to feel lonesome. He wished he knew some guys in New York so he could hang around with them and fill up the time from three until dinner.

Then one day Mr. Hart started work on a new social studies project. He said Americans lived in a time when a lot of people weren't happy with their country's leaders. He said people felt that way before 1776 too, and that it was important for them to study about the American Revolution. The class formed committees to study, talk, and make reports. Jeffrey got on the Causes of the Revolution Committee with Santos, Patty, Suzanne, Herbert, and a black kid named Matthew.

Patty spoke up a lot in class and she got to be head of the committee. She called a meeting right after school in Central Park. They played ball and clowned around awhile and then they sat on the grass near a big old tree. Jeffrey had never seen so many big trees before he moved here. All the Lakeview trees were little and new.

Patty said she thought the Causes of the Revolution Committee should split up into teams and do separate reports. Everyone said okay, they would meet again in a week or two and work on their big report. Jeffrey and Matthew were picked to do the Boston Tea Party, and Matthew wanted to get started right away.

They walked down a path in the park and Jeffrey saw some people riding bikes. He hadn't been on his since he had moved. Frank the doorman was a good guy and had found a place for the bike in the basement. Sometimes Jeffrey would go down and sit next to his bike for awhile, but he hadn't ridden it till now. Matthew said he didn't know how to ride and besides they had to go to the library, but Jeffrey said they could ride together, and wasn't there a library on another side of the park. Matthew knew all about all of the libraries in the city and said there was one across town.

Jeffrey took Matthew to his house, got the bike, and walked to the bicycle path. Matthew rode the handlebars, and Jeffrey pedaled down the road, through the long winding green park, as a soft autumn wind blew the first leaves down from the trees.

Later, when Jeffrey told Mom about Matthew and the other kids on his committee, she said, "That's nice," but she didn't really seem to hear at all. Jeffrey counted the days till Sunday when he could tell his father all about his new friends. When Sunday came he got up early and was all ready before noon. His mother spent all morning combing her hair and putting stuff on her eyes. He felt she looked in the mirror more than she did at him. When she finished dressing she looked like an actress on television. She didn't look like his mother at all.

At twelve she started watching the clock and saying, "Where is he?" She walked around the apartment from the clock to the telephone and she had her hand on the receiver when it rang. Jeffrey heard her say, "What do you mean you can't make it today? I have plans. A woman I work with invited me to a party. I must start to get out and meet new people."

She kept on talking for a few minutes in the same low voice and then she said, "He's right here," and called Jeffrey to the phone.

Jeffrey listened as his dad said, "We'll make up for it next Sunday," and he answered, "Sure, Dad," and tried to make his voice smile, but when

he hung up he could hardly keep the tears back. Another whole week. It had been such a long time since last week.

"He promised to come every Sunday," Jeff said, half to himself and half to his mother.

"When did that man ever keep his promises?" his mother said. She bit her lip, put her arm around his shoulder, and made her voice sound happy. "Well, Jeff, it looks like it's you and me today. We'll think of something exciting to do, just the two of us, and next week your dad will be here for sure."

She went into her room and looked up a number in the little book she always carried in her purse. Then the telephone rang again and Jeffrey picked it up.

"Oh, hi, Matthew," he said. "Yeah, that sounds great. Hold on a minute. I'll ask Mom."

He ran to his mother. "Mom," he said, "Matthew wants to work on our report. He wants me to come to his house for lunch and then we can take a bus to the library. You know what? Matthew knows a library that's open on Sundays. He says they have all kinds of books to study from and they only let you in if you're a kid."

"Matthew," his mother said. "Is that your

partner on the committee, the boy you told me about?"

"Yeah, that's the kid. And he wants to show me the great big library on Fifth Avenue first. He says I can look at the big one from the outside, and then we can walk over to the one that's open. Can I tell him okay?"

Mom still held the little red address book. She ran her thumb over it. "I guess it's okay, dear," she said. "Don't be out too late."

Matthew's house smelled good and felt warm. Matthew had a mother and a father, and a big sister and a baby brother. Everyone talked and laughed a lot. Matthew's mother kept putting more food on Jeffrey's plate and saying, "My goodness, child, you don't hardly eat enough to keep a bird alive."

When it was time to go Jeffrey didn't want to leave. He felt like staying in Matthew's house for a long time. Matthew's mother said Jeffrey was a very good boy and asked why he hadn't come around before. Jeffrey said they had just moved here.

"We moved to this house last year," Matthew said. "My mama and papa wanted us to live in this neighborhood. They said it's good for all different kinds of people to live near each other."

"That's right, sugar," Matthew's mother said. "Is that why your mama and papa moved?"

Jeffry shook his head. "My folks are getting divorced. I live with my mom."

Matthew's mother nodded slowly and went into the kitchen. She came back with a handful of warm cookies for Jeffrey and Matthew. She said it was so they wouldn't get hungry on the bus. She gave Matthew a great big hug. She hugged Jeffrey too and said, "You come again real soon, hear?"

Matthew and Jeffrey ate their cookies as the bus rode through the park on the way downtown. Matthew rang the buzzer and the bus stopped in front of a big building with stone lions out in front. They got off the bus and stood looking up at the tall flight of high steps that led to the biggest library Jeffrey had ever seen. Then they walked up streets lined with people window-shopping, until at last they came to the special Sunday library.

The time between school and dinner started to grow shorter. Jeffrey walked with Matthew after school or played ball with the kids or rode his bike in the park. The whole week seemed shorter and Sunday came more quickly. This time his

father really came. He came early, laughing and talking in a happy voice, and with a package hidden behind his back.

Jeffrey opened the package and found a brand-new baseball glove. Next to a cork wall near his bed, what Jeffrey wanted most of all was a glove. He got so excited he ran to his dad and hugged him.

"Listen, Jeffrey," Dad said, "that's only the first surprise. For my next surprise we get into my car, drive to Mapleton Lanes, have some lunch, bowl a few games, and go to Aunt Anita's for dinner." Dad picked up Jeffrey and swung him around in the air like he had when Jeffrey was little. Lakeview. Jeffrey hadn't been back there since he moved. He could see Wayne again, and Mark, and his old house. He whirled around in the air dizzily and held his father around the neck.

"You know, Dad," Jeffrey said, "I wish every day was Sunday. I wish for a whole week of Sundays." He got back down, his head still spinning around. "No, Dad," he said, "you know what? I wish for a whole month of Sundays."

As the car rode down the long highway, Jeff looked out the window and dreamed. His father was taking him back to Lakeview. Maybe that was because he missed him so much. Maybe that meant they were going to buy their old house again and he was going back to live with his mom and dad. Maybe that was his father's next surprise. They were going back to Lakeview for good.

When they got to Lakeview they passed Wayne's house first.

"Dad," Jeffrey said, "let's ask Wayne to come along."

Dad said, "Sure, pal," and Jeff was out of the car before it stopped.

"Hey, Wayne," he called, "come on! We're going bowling."

Wayne ran out. "Hey, old buddy," he said, "how you been?"

"Good," Jeff said. "My dad is out in the car. Hop in. We're going to Mapleton."

Wayne said, "Gee, I can't. We're going to visit my aunt and uncle in Plainfield. They had some old baby or something." Then Wayne's folks came out, and they all got into their own car and rode away. "Call me, huh?" Wayne said, waving from the car window.

Jeffrey's dad drove by Glen's house but there was nobody home and nobody answered Mark's bell either. When they came to his old block, Jeffrey waited for his father to stop the car in front of the house. But he didn't even slow down. Jeffrey sat on his knees and leaned out the car window as far as he could so he wouldn't miss his house, but when they got there only the street-lamp on the lawn told him it was 801. His house was painted yellow and the shutters were green. Jeffrey could see people moving around his back-yard and a man in a high white hat stood near a new barbecue pit. Jeffrey thought of his white house with the black shutters. He sat back down in his seat and looked away even before they passed Hillcrest Lane.

Bowling at Mapleton Lanes wasn't the same anymore either. Jeff always used to have a good time with his dad. His dad acted happy most of the time and they always had fun together, but sometimes there were quiet times, too. Now his dad kept talking all the time, buying candy, buying sodas, and saying, "Having a good time, Jeff?" and "Isn't this fun, pal?"

Later, at Aunt Anita's, it was more like family, even though Mom wasn't there. Jeff would have had a better time at his aunt's if she didn't keep shoving food at him and if everybody didn't keep cheerfully asking him every minute how he was doing, like he had the measles or something.

Sometimes, at the dinner table, and later even after dinner, he would look up and catch Aunt Anita or Uncle Bert or Aunt Carolyn staring at him. Then they would do what grown-ups seemed to do lots of times — talk around you like you weren't there. They talked to each other in low tones, figuring it was too low for you to hear, or figuring you weren't paying attention, or they used big words, figuring you wouldn't be able to tell what they were talking about.

He heard Aunt Anita's low voice saying, "The boy seems so unhappy. Can't you do anything?"

He heard his father say, "Believe me, I wish I could. I'm trying as hard as I can to cheer him up. But it's rough on the kid."

Aunt Anita whispered something else, and his father said, "Rough on me, too. Sometimes things just get away from you."

Uncle Bert talked in a low voice and Jeff heard the words, ". . . patch things up" and ". . . can't you try again?"

Dad's voice got lower but Jeff caught, "People marry so young, they don't really know each other," and ". . . gone too far to turn back," and "We tried."

Jeffrey woke up a few times that night, thinking it was time to go to school, but the alarm was quiet and the room was dark. Pictures of the yellow house with the green shutters kept flashing in his mind. But maybe that was why his dad didn't stop the car. Maybe he was saving the surprise for next week. Till the man with the barbecue pit could move, and till his dad could paint their house white again and the shutters black.

Next morning Jeffrey woke up tired. He walked to school slowly and when he got to the yard his whole committee crowded around him.

"Jeffrey," Herbert cried, "we're having a block party on our street this Saturday. They're closing the street to traffic just for us."

"That's beautiful," Jeffrey said. He looked around the group. Herbert lived down the street. "But what about the other kids?" he said. "Patty and Matthew and everybody?"

"Oh, we can bring some friends," Herbert answered. "You bring some and I'll bring some and our whole committee can come."

"That's great," Patty said. "Do you want us to help?"

Herbert said that everybody was bringing something to eat. "My mom is making her own gefilte fish," he said proudly.

"I'll tell my mama," Matthew said. "She'll fix something, too."

Jeffrey thought of the great big cake with icing and coconut on top that Mom made whenever company came and when somebody had a birthday. "I'll tell my mother to bake a cake," he said.

That night he ran to meet his mother when she came home from work. He told her all about the block party even before the door closed behind her.

She said, "That's nice, dear," and sat down tiredly.

"I said you'd bake us a cake," he said. "You know, the one with the coconut on it."

"Oh, no, Jeff," she sighed, kicking off her shoes. "That cake takes days to make. I'd have to shop for the ingredients and I'm too tired after working all day."

"You're always tired," he burst out. "You never do anything anymore. You don't care about me."

"Stop feeling sorry for yourself," she said.

"I'll call Matthew," he said angrily. "His mom will make something for me to bring. She's a real mother."

"I'll bet Matthew wouldn't act this way. I'll bet he doesn't talk that way to his mother."

"I hate you," he screamed. "You made me move and you took away my daddy."

He looked at the woman in the long earrings and remembered her in a pretty apron moving around their kitchen in Lakeview. He got mad at the tears for starting to come and he blinked them back hard.

"You're not my mother anymore," he yelled, and he ran from the room, slammed the outside door as hard as he could, and rushed into the waiting elevator.

"Well, come on in, Jeffrey," Matthew's mother said. "Matthew's not home just now, but come right on into the kitchen."

"Where'd Matthew go, Mrs. Walters?" Jeffrey asked.

"He's at the library. You know my boy — get him near a book and he loses all track of time. He'll be home soon though, and we'll eat when Papa wakes up from his nap. Can you stay for supper? There's plenty of stew."

Jeffrey shook his head. "I'm not very hungry."

"Well you just sit yourself down at the table while I stir the stew. Matthew will be back any minute now."

"Mrs. Walters," Jeff said quickly, the words tumbling out, "can you fix me something for the block party Saturday? I asked my mom and she said she didn't want to do it. She said she was too tired. She never cares anything about me anymore. I want you to be my mother. I don't ever want to go back to her again."

Matthew's mother looked at Jeffrey, dipped a spoon into the steaming pot and put some stew on a plate.

"Now you just taste a little of this. You'll feel better. I have to see to the baby for a second, and then I'll be right back and we'll talk."

Mrs. Walters left the room, came back, and sat down at the table. "How was the stew, honey?" she said.

"Good. I wish I had a mother who cooked. A real mother like Matthew does."

Mrs. Walters put some more stew on Jeffrey's plate. "Did Matthew tell you I was his real mother?"

Jeffrey looked up. "What do you mean, Mrs. Walters?"

"Well, Jeffrey," she said slowly, "sometimes things aren't what they seem. I'm Matthew's mama now, but I wasn't always. I took Matthew from the children's shelter two years ago. He doesn't even know who his real folks were. I'm his real mama now, for sure, but Matthew didn't have a mama or a papa for a long, long time." She put her hand on Jeffrey's shoulder. "But you always had a real mama and papa," she said gently. "You still have both of them, even if they're not together anymore."

Jeffrey put down his spoon. He sat still while Mrs. Walters' words sank in.

"But my mother doesn't care," he said. "She wouldn't even make me anything for the block party."

"Wouldn't, baby?" Matthew's mother said gently. "Wouldn't, or couldn't? She works all day. And, besides, it's caring, not cooking, that makes a real mama. It's not the same for your mama now. She's got to get used to the idea that there's no papa in her house anymore either."

Jeffrey looked down at his plate.

"That takes a lot of getting used to," she said.

46

"Just like seeing your papa only every Sunday takes a lot of getting used to. But you've still got your mama and you've still got your papa, your very own flesh and blood."

Jeffrey's cheeks felt wet. Mrs. Walters hugged him to her. "Don't you think you'd best be getting home now, sugar?" Mrs. Walters said. "Your mama must be worried half to death."

Jeffrey thought of Matthew in a children's shelter, growing up with no one to love him, and he hugged Mrs. Walters back.

The door was open when Jeffrey got home. He walked in quietly and found his mom in his room, walking up and down. She ran to him and hugged him long and hard.

"Oh, Jeff," she cried, "I love you so much. I was worried sick till Mrs. Walters called."

"I didn't know she called," Jeff said. He thought of the few minutes when she had gone to care for the baby.

"Yes, darling. I wanted to run right over and get you, but Mrs. Walters said it might be better if you stayed awhile and had a bite to eat. She said she'd call again if she needed me. She seems like a wonderful woman. I'm looking forward to meeting her at the block party."

"You'll come?"

"You couldn't keep me away." She laughed and hugged him again. "You know, Jeff, *I* miss Lakeview too, sometimes."

Jeffrey nodded. "I know. Mrs. Walters said there's no daddy in your house either."

"That's right. Things are different for me, too, Jeff. I have to build a new life now. I couldn't do that back in Lakeview. That's one reason why we moved to New York. I'm uprooted too, Jeff, just like you are. We're going to have to grow together, honey, starting now." She held his face in her hands and smiled. "Now, how about you going to the market for me after school Friday? I'll write a list. Then I'll bake our cake after work Friday and we'll frost it Saturday morning. You can even lick the spoon, okay?"

He nodded. "Sure, Mom," he said. "I'll help too."

"That's my big son," she said, and sat down on the chair near his bed. She looked at the carton that stood on the floor near the closet. Everything from his old cork wall was still packed.

"Jeff honey," she said, "the stores are open late Thursday and we're having dinner downtown and going shopping!" She reached into the carton, picked up the Little League trophy and held it in both hands. "We'll look together and we'll keep looking till we make sure we pick out the nicest wall bulletin board in town."

The week was very busy and went by quickly. Mom's special cake was ready early Saturday morning, and when Jeffrey took it downstairs he hardly knew the block. Streamers ran across fire escapes and hung throughout the street. There were balloons in all colors and cardboard flowers all over. Tables covered with paper tablecloths and filled with all kinds of different dishes were set up on both sides of the street.

Jeffrey spotted Herbert and took his cake to the table. Herbert's mother had made gefilte fish and a sweet noodle pudding. Matthew's mother had made fried chicken and a sweet-potato pie. Patty brought a large dish of lasagna, Suzanne came with Swedish meatballs, and Santos brought rice and beans.

Music started playing and Jeffrey saw a real band with all their instruments right outside. They played soul music, rock music, and Spanish music, and little kids, mothers, fathers, grandmas, and grandpas clapped as teen-agers danced in the middle of the street.

Jeffrey clapped to the music, played games with the kids, and kept filling his plate. His mom laughed and asked where he was putting it all, but she was having a good time too, and she let him taste anything he wanted to. When it got dark, the best party Jeffrey had ever been to was almost over, and he went upstairs with his mom. He felt tired and good all over, even in the place where his stomach hurt.

When Dad came next day Jeffrey told him all about the block party. Dad said that was great and that they were going to have a wonderful time

today, too. He said they would try to get tickets to a matinee at the rodeo and then they would go out to eat at someplace real fancy.

Jeff thought of the Sundays back in Lakeview when his dad would sit on the lawn reading the paper. Jeff would come and stand nearby and Dad would put the paper down and they would sit and talk. Sometimes they would just toss a ball back and forth on the lawn and fool around till dinnertime.

"Dad," Jeff said, "we're going to see a ball game next week. Can't we just go to the park today and play catch?"

"Play catch?" his father said. "I thought we'd do something extra special."

"We're always doing something extra special. We didn't used to. We're always watching things lately, Dad. We never do anything anymore." He looked away. "Sometimes I feel like you're divorcing me too."

Dad put his arm around Jeffrey. "You know, that's why I keep wanting to do something special. To make up for the rest of the week because I miss you so much. Sometimes I feel like I have a Sunday son and it's not easy." Jeff leaned his head against his father's chest. "But you're my boy and you always will be, even when you're tall as I am, and I'll always love you just the same."

Jeff waited for the lump in his throat to melt and go away. "I love you, too, Dad," he said.

His dad lifted him and hugged him in the air. "I guess that's special enough for any Sunday," he said quietly. He put Jeff down and squeezed his shoulder. "Go get your new baseball glove, pal, and we'll go out and toss a few."

When he got back, his mother was waiting for him. "Look, Jeff, I went for a ride in the country to see the leaves turning and brought back some fresh apple cider. Let's have some."

"Great, Mom," he said and walked straight to the kitchen.

Mom poured some cider and put out a plate of doughnuts. "What did you and Dad do today, Jeff?" she asked.

"Oh, Mom," he said, "we went to Central Park and played catch. Then we had lunch right outside the park. Dad bought hot dogs from the man who has the stand with the striped umbrella on top. I had my hot dog with onions and mustard and sauerkraut. Dad got me a chocolate drink too. And we sat on a bench and ate and talked.

We had such a swell Sunday. It was the greatest."

She stood in back of him and hugged him around the neck. "I'm so glad, Jeff," she said.

They sat at the table together, eating their doughnuts and drinking their cider. And then the phone rang and Mom went to answer it. She came back into the kitchen. "It's your friend Matthew, honey."

Jeff picked up the phone and said, "Hi, Matthew."

"I waited till now to call you because I know your papa comes on Sunday," Matthew said. "The kids on our committee came over to my house today. We're all going to bring food and have a picnic in Central Park next Saturday. We'll talk about our report and then we're going to the planetarium and the Museum of Natural History. They've got real dinosaurs there."

"Great. Say, Matthew, why doesn't everybody come over here and fix the picnic lunch? Mom will help. Some of the kids haven't been to my house yet."

"Sure," Matthew said, "we'll all bring something and meet at your house."

Jeffrey said, "That's beautiful," and when he

hung up he went back to the kitchen, finished his cider and doughnut, and told his mother about next Saturday. They were still sitting in the kitchen when the phone rang again. Jeffrey answered it.

"Hi, Jeff, old buddy," Wayne's voice said. "Who you been talking to? Your line's been busy all night."

"Hi, Wayne," Jeff said. "I was talking to my friend Matthew."

"Oh. Say listen, Jeff. Next Saturday's my birthday. I'm having a party and everyone will be there. Can you come?"

"Gee, Wayne," Jeff said, "Matthew called about Saturday too. Our committee is meeting."

"Some old school committee," Wayne said. "Can't you get out of it? Or do you have a teacher like Mrs. Woodruff?"

"No," Jeff said, "Mr. Hart is my teacher. He's got long hair and a beard and he drives his motorcycle to school every day."

"No kidding," Wayne said. "Gee, that's cool."

"Yeah," Jeff said. "And we have all kinds of kids in my class. We had a block party last week with Spanish food and soul food and everything."

Jeff was starting to feel very grown up and important. "And Saturday everybody's bringing food and we're having a picnic in Central Park. Then after we have our meeting we're going to the planetarium and see the stars and planets. We're going through the Museum of Natural History, too. Matthew says they've got real dinosaurs there."

"Wow, that's terrific," Wayne said. "I wish I was on your committee. I guess you don't want to break that date to come to some old birthday party."

Jeff stayed quiet a minute, and all at once he knew that Wayne was right. He didn't want to break it, not even if he could. He wanted to go to see the stars, and see the dinosaurs, and have a picnic with his friends, right here in Central Park, right here in New York.

"Gee," he said, so Wayne wouldn't feel bad, "I hate to miss your party. I wish it was some other day, so I could come and see you, and see our whole gang."

"Yeah," Wayne said, "but your dad comes every week. Can't you tell him to drive you out to Lakeview Sunday?"

"We've got tickets to a ball game next Sunday," Jeff said, "but I'll call you and we'll make it for another week."

"Okay, old buddy," Wayne said. "There'll be other Sundays."

"Sure, Wayne," Jeff said, "see you soon. There'll be lots and lots of Sundays."

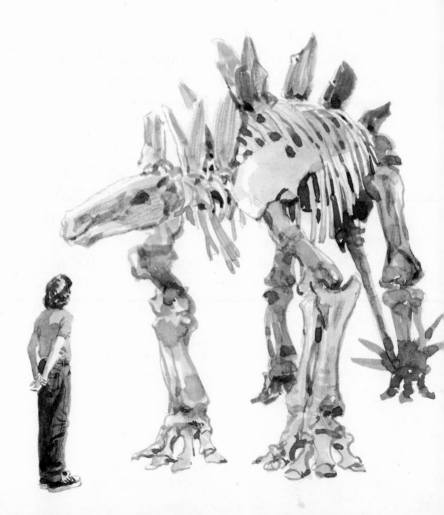